About the Book

This is the story of a musical genius. Stevie Wonder was born blind. His parents separated when he was very young, and his mother moved to a rundown section of Detroit. Stevie was poor, and he couldn't see— but he could hear the world, and he was happy. He began making music when he was three—singing and playing the piano and beating on pots and pans. When he was ten he was discovered by Motown—and by the time he was twelve he had written and recorded "Fingertips," which sold over one and a half million records.

Today, Stevie Wonder is one of our best loved and most respected young composers and musicians. His music, his special Wonder music, brings joy to people all over the world.

A See and Read Biography

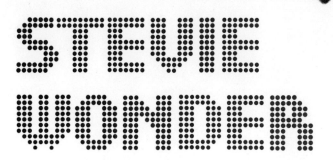

STEVIE WONDER

by Beth P. Wilson

illustrated by James Calvin

G.P. Putnam's Sons · New York

Library of Congress Cataloging in Publication Data
Wilson, Beth P.
Stevie Wonder.
(A See and read biography)
SUMMARY: A Biography of the blind composer,
pianist, and singer whose musical ability, apparent
since childhood, has earned him many awards.
1. Wonder, Stevie—Juvenile literature. 2. Rock
musicians—United States—Biography—Juvenile litera-
ture. [1. Wonder, Stevie. 2. Musicians. 3. Afro-
Americans—Biography] I. Calvin, James. II. Title.
ML3930.W65W54   784'.092'4 [B] [92]   78-6054
ISBN 0-399-61106-1

To
Aisha Zakiya and Keita Sawandi
the children of Stevie and Yolanda

A group of boys raced down the street.

They were going to hear their friend Stevie give a concert in the mini-park by their school. Eight-year-old Stevie was already playing his harmonica when they got there. He was swaying back and forth with the music.

Girls and boys crowded around when he beat on his bongo drums. Some of them danced and clapped with the rhythm. When Stevie began singing, his friends called out, "You're a real music man!"

"I like to make music," he called back.

Stevie was born Steveland Morris in Saginaw, Michigan, on May 13, 1950. When he was a small boy, his parents separated. His mother, Mrs. Lulu Mae Hardaway, moved her family of six children to Detroit. They lived in a rundown part of the city and they had little money. The children did not see their father often, so Mrs. Hardaway took care of them alone.

Stevie was born blind. Many times his mother took him to doctors for help. But each time the doctors told her they couldn't make Stevie see. Then Mrs. Hardaway took Stevie to faith healers, who touched his eyes and prayed for him. But they couldn't make Stevie see, either.

Mrs. Hardaway worried about Stevie. She wanted to take special care of him. She tried to protect Stevie as he moved about. But Stevie was too curious and lively to stay with his mother all the time. He didn't want to miss anything. He ran about with other children, and he rode a bicycle with his brother Calvin steering.

One day he climbed a tree to feel the swirling air. He whispered to himself, "If I could see for one minute, I could see the whole world. Whatever I saw that one minute would be the whole world."

But Stevie heard the world—children laughing on the block, birds chirping in the park, splashing water and barking dogs. He heard the honking horns and the rolling of heavy truck tires. And he heard calm, sweet voices as well as harsh, angry words. But the songs he heard on the radio were his favorite sounds.

From the time Stevie was two years old, he marched about the house beating pots and pans in time to music. One day when he was three, he ran to the piano. Standing on tiptoe to reach the keys, he played music. Mrs. Hardaway called the other children to see him. They could hardly believe it.

When Stevie was five, an uncle gave him his first harmonica. He wore it on a chain around his neck. Stevie played it every chance he could. Later, he got a larger harmonica. And when Stevie was

nine, he was given a drum with two sticks, called a snare drum. It came from an organization to help blind children.

He spent hours playing his harmonica and his drum. And at Sunday school he swayed with the gospel songs. Stevie thought he might like to become a minister when he grew up.

Stevie listened to the Black radio station in Detroit. Sometimes he played his harmonica with the music. This station played the music of B. B. King and other rhythm and blues artists. The blind musician Ray Charles became his idol. He remembers how excited he was when he had his picture taken with this musical genius.

After school, Stevie would sit on the back steps and play his harmonica or his bongo drums. All kinds of melodies came to him. He could play one tune after another. Sometimes the family would come out to listen, or Stevie would give a home concert for his friends.

When a neighbor noticed how much time Stevie spent with his music, she told Stevie's mother that he could use her piano. Mrs. Hardaway thanked the neighbor, because they no longer had a piano.

Now Stevie could play his harmonica, his drums, and the piano. He kept weaving new harmonies. Sometimes words came to him along with the music. When the neighbor moved away, she gave her piano to Stevie.

Stevie went to public school with other boys and girls. His brother Calvin walked to school with him, and at recess he took

Stevie to the playground. Stevie made friends easily, and he was a good student.

Because he was blind, most people thought of Stevie as a little Black boy with big problems. But Stevie remembers his childhood as a happy time.

One of his songs tells how much fun his family had together, even at Christmas when the children received only a few toys. When Stevie was very young, he usually got a tin drum with a cardboard top that he beat to pieces in a short time.

When Stevie was ten years old, Ronnie White, a singer in the popular group called The Miracles, heard about him from his younger brother. His brother and his friends kept saying, "You should hear him. He sings and plays and beats the drums!"

After Mr. White had heard this enough times, he decided to listen to Stevie. The boys were right. Stevie made music in a special way. He sang out with his own kind of beat and rhythm.

Mr. White took Stevie to Hitsville, U. S. A., in Detroit. This was

the name of a Black company that made records. He introduced Stevie to Mr. Berry Gordy, Jr., the president of the company. Stevie played songs written by others and music of his own. Mr. Gordy listened to Stevie and liked what he heard. He wanted to give Stevie a contract to make records for five years.

Because Stevie was so young, he needed a "legal guardian." His guardian would take care of the business details and watch out for Stevie. It was important that Stevie stay in school and be with his family and friends like any other boy his age. His guardian would see that Stevie could do this and make music. By this time, Stevie had already written his first song, "Lonely Boy."

When Stevie was twelve years old, he composed a song called "Fingertips." At the studio, Stevie sang and played as the music was put on tape. Then the notes were taken from tape, and the song was made into a record. On one side of the record Stevie played "Finger-tips" on his harmonica while a band played in the background. On the other side of the record Stevie sang the song.

After the record was made, people in the studio stood about talking and congratulating him. Stevie found himself laughing and talking because of the warm feeling of success. He was excited to be around people who liked and recorded his music.

"Fingertips" sold over one and a half million records. Stevie was a hit. All the radio stations played "Fingertips." It was number one in popularity around the country. People began talking about this boy. Mr. Gordy named his young musician "Little Stevie Wonder." And he changed his company's name to Motown.

Music lovers came to Stevie's concerts. They wanted to see and hear this boy wonder. Soon people were saying, "Oh yes, Stevie Wonder—Motown."

Still, Stevie lived as normal a life as possible. He got good grades in school. After supper he did his lessons and read from his braille Bible, made especially for the blind. He still rode his bike with Calvin, and he liked fooling around with his friends in the neighborhood. He told them jokes, and stories about people he met. And he told them how he made records.

Sometimes he got into trouble when he and his pals did things like writing names on doors and walls. Once he slipped out the back door when his mother told him to stay inside. That was fun until his mother found out about it. .

Because of school, Stevie gave concerts on weekends and during vacations. When he traveled, he would ask someone to take him shopping. Even though his weekly allowance was only $2.50, he always bought a present for his mother and one for his baby sister, Renée. Motown gave his family money for his expenses. The rest

went into a bank. This money would be his to use when he grew up.

When it was time to go to high school, Stevie enrolled at the Michigan School for the Blind in Lansing. There he learned to read music in braille. He took lessons in piano, violin, and string bass. He played bass in the school orchestra.

And, at Lansing, he learned to swim and to wrestle. When Stevie swam, the cool lapping water against his body made him feel fresh and calm. When he wrestled, he liked the strong tug of his body against the other boy's. Stevie made many friends in high school.

During the summer months, Stevie gave concerts to screaming, enthusiastic crowds of fans. He worked with some of the best musicians of popular music in the country. And he learned a lot from them. Stevie was moving ahead fast.

But he remembered what it was like growing up in a poor neighborhood. He knew he must get a good education, no matter what he planned to do. A teacher traveled with him, and he was able to keep up with his schoolwork.

By the time Stevie Wonder was seventeen years old, he had written a number of songs. Some were on small records called "singles." Each side of a single has only one song. Others were on large records called "albums." There are several songs on each side of an album. The label in the center of each record told who wrote the words and music for the songs.

Hit songs kept coming from Stevie. Everything he wrote seemed to be what his fans wanted. Some songs made people want to dance because of the beat. Others had lovely, slow melodies that made people sit and listen and dream.

One album, called "For Once in My Life," included Stevie's songs and the songs of other famous musicians. One of Stevie's numbers was the bubbly song "Shoo-Be-Do-Be-Doo-Da-Day," and another was called "I'm More Than Happy." Stevie played all the numbers in the album with great feeling.

By this time Stevie Wonder had played all over America and in Europe. This meant moving from city to city and from hotel to hotel. It meant big stages, bright lights, and meeting lots of strangers. Stevie realized how much work it took to get ready for concerts in different cities. He had to learn many things at a young age.

LONDON

PARIS

When traveling in Europe, Stevie got to know people of different nationalities, their languages, and the way they lived. Traveling gave him much to think and write about. He knew what life should be like. He wanted people to be kind to one another. Once he said if he could see some of the crime and hatred, perhaps he would not be able to write beautiful music. He would be too angry about what he saw.

ROME

In 1969 Stevie graduated with honors from the Michigan School for the Blind. Now he could spend all of his time with music. And he needed every minute. So many words and melodies came to him that he scarcely had time to put them down. Sometimes he worked late into the night. Other times he would get up early in the morning and start composing.

Stevie Wonder was now a young man making music that was not just pop or soul. It was "Wonder" music, sometimes with a happy bounce and sometimes with a slow, dreamy tempo. Stevie did

not worry about matching words
with notes. He just sang out the
story he wanted to tell. Sometimes
he would call out in the middle of
a song. Or he might repeat some of
the words over and over again.

Stevie's new sound was different from the Motown sound, which was popular and easy to recognize. His music was growing and changing. His compositions were richer and more varied. Sometimes one could hear the influence of other cultures in the instruments he used. More than ever Stevie's music was his own original Wonder music.

Stevie was happy with his music, but Motown was not pleased with the change. They wanted to do what they knew was successful. Stevie wanted to grow. He wanted to be able to choose his own musicians and others who worked with him in the studio. He wanted the freedom to express in his music the joy and magic he felt, and to break away from the familiar Motown sound. Stevie insisted on a new contract, and in 1972 he and Motown signed one.

In 1971 Stevie Wonder was twenty-one years old. He was given all the money he had earned from the time he was a child. Soon Stevie left his home and moved to New York City. There he began to experiment with new sounds. He wrote and produced music the way he wanted it to be. And he started playing all the instruments he wanted to use in his songs—piano, harmonica, bass, and clarinet.

Stevie was now using an instrument called a Moog and Arp synthesizer along with his own singing and playing. This machine had a simple keyboard. It was made so it could play back the sounds of musical instruments. Sometimes the sounds of ten or twelve instruments could be heard at the same time. Stevie called it his dream machine because, he said, it helped him to express the full beauty of his melodies.

Stevie's new music talked about many things. He wrote a question and answer song called "Black Man." Stevie asked the questions and children called out the answers. He said all people had done important things—the Red man, the Black man, the Brown man, the White man, and the Yellow man. And he said,

"It's time we learned
   This world was made for all
   men."

Stevie also wrote new love songs. People needed to be kind to each other. They needed to learn to love one another. He said the whole wide world needed love today.

All was going well. His new music was successful. Then, in August, 1973, Stevie was injured in an automobile accident on a highway near Durham, North Carolina. Stevie Wonder lay in a hospital bed unable to move or to speak.

LONDON

People everywhere prayed and waited. His friend Ira Tucker, Jr. sat by his bed. He whispered in Stevie's ear. Then he sang words from one of Stevie's albums. Slowly Stevie began to move his fingers. His body moved a little. He was going to live!

After seven months, Stevie was well and ready for concerts again. He traveled to England, to France, and back to the United States. All the tickets to his concerts were sold in a few hours. Great crowds cheered him and wanted to shake his hand wherever he went.

Stevie Wonder was a different young man after his accident. He appreciated the beauty of life more than ever, but he was lonely. He wanted to share his life with someone. Soon he fell in love with a young woman named Yolanda. And Yolanda fell in love with Stevie. They were happy together and had two children, Aisha and Keita. One of his songs, "Isn't She Lovely?" is about the birth of his daughter Aisha.

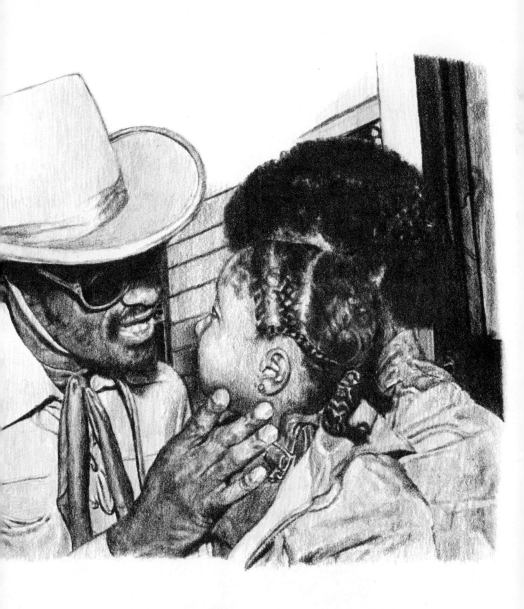

Stevie was thankful for all the good things that had happened to him. Even though he was busy working on an important new album, he stopped long enough to go where he was needed. He gave concerts to raise money for people who needed help.

One was a special Christmas program in New York City for older people who needed better

living conditions. Another was for
special programs to help children
who had trouble learning their
school lessons. He also gave a concert in San Francisco for the National Newspaper Publishers. The
money from this concert went to
help students who wanted to become newspaper writers.

In May, 1975, Stevie Wonder became the special guest at the Human Kindness Day Program in Washington, D.C. Stevie received his award for being such a fine musician and for helping people in any way he could. In accepting the award he said, "As I always say, I am thankful." That evening he gave a free concert on the Washington Monument grounds. More than fifty thousand people were there.

In 1976 the Stevie Wonder Home for Blind and Retarded Children in Lansing, Michigan, was opened. Stevie had given the money for this home. He knew that everybody has trouble from time to time. And some have big problems. So he and his brother Calvin wrote a song called "Have a Talk With God." Part of it says

"When you feel your life's too
    hard
Just go have a talk with God—
Just go talk to God, He cares.
I know he does."

This lovely song came from his 1976 double-album, "Songs in the Key of Life," that won so many awards.

Then, in January, 1977, Stevie, in African dress, was playing at a big festival in Lagos, Nigeria, in West Africa. He was told by telephone that he had won special honors at the American Music Awards in California. Again, in January, 1978, he won two awards at this program. He had now sold over forty million records. He had received the "Ebby" at the Ebony Music Awards, and the top artist award from Billboard No. 1 Music Awards.

These awards represented just one more recognition for this young musical genius, Stevie Wonder, whose music continues to touch people all around the world.

About the Author

BETH P. WILSON was born and raised in Tacoma, Washington, and was graduated from the University of Puget Sound. She currently serves as an educational consultant in the California public school system.

Mrs. Wilson has been writing since she was a very small child. Her most recent biography for Putnam's, *Muhammad Ali*, was selected by the National Council of Social Studies/Children's Book Council joint committee as one of the Notable Children's Trade Books in the Field of Social Studies.

Mrs. Wilson and her husband live in Berkeley, California.

ABOUT THE ARTIST

JAMES CALVIN received his B.F.A. from the Rochester Institute of Technology and his M.F.A. from New York University. He has illustrated a number of children's books and has had several one-man shows of paintings and prints. He currently teaches a Media Arts course at Malcolm-King College in New York.

Mr. Calvin was born in Saginaw, Michigan, in 1950—the place and year of Stevie Wonder's birth—and has a special affinity for his subject. He now lives in New York City.